Circles of Gold

(a fable)

Shunned by all,
would he ever be accepted?

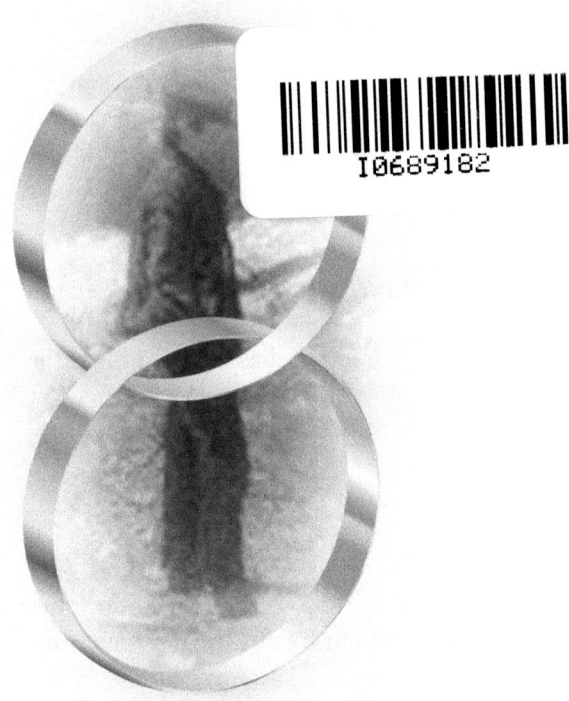

Philip J Bradbury

Circles of Gold
(a fable)

Philip J Bradbury

Published by   The Write Site,
                Brisbane, Australia

Copyright 2016 © Philip J Bradbury

www.philipjbradbury.com

Philip J Bradbury has asserted his right under
the Copyright, Designs and Patents Act 1988
to be identified as the author.

ISBN- 978-0-9922908-8-7

What readers are saying ...

Your writing has rhythm and you build good climaxes through your language. You've definitely got the fire and brimstone side of it down and it can be pretty powerful stuff.

~ Nomadagio

I really enjoyed this story. I liked the way that the father had to deal with his own emotions concerning the birth deformities of his son, and his role as a priest in life. The story moved along at a good pace and I was entertained throughout.

~ John

The story is well-written and draws the reader in. The narrative is well-written. You write well and your dialogue (although lengthy) is good.

~ Colin Davy

This was a lovely story. I was thoroughly entertained and my interest was held right through. It is a beautiful fairy story to me or rather I should write, mythical. The settings were vivid and so visual I could almost imagine I was walking alongside the horse and then the cart. The dialogue was clear and sharp and did not jar. There was also the subtext of deformity which was Alfred Adler's (one of Freud's disciples) theory of neurosis. You executed this very well. The ending ... was touching and so original. Great story.

~ KatyXY

There are almost always positive things to say about a piece of writing to quote the fine print. It is rare to find a piece that one can say only positive things as is the case here.

Also it is rare to find a story which has been so beautifully written. I use 'beautifully' rather than well written because your use of the language is outstanding it starts at the first sentence the first 'Once upon a time, when dreaming was useful, a child was born' and runs all the way through the story to 'They smiled at each other as he urged Clyde to start for the village. He shyly put his hand on hers and she didn't move hers away.'

~ Harry Helfer

A good read which held my attention to the end. I liked the way the story moved along and enjoyed getting to know your character. I really enjoyed this story. I thought the character was well developed and believable. The pace was just right for this type of narrative, and kept my interest.

~ Colleen S

Philip, I found this story quite endearing. I was expecting a horrible deformity and when I read it was a golden belly button, I couldn't help but laugh. Of all the things to be upset about? You managed to portray his father's sentiment about it. The ending was lovely and, overall, I found it to be a nice read.

~ Gabriella

This reads like a classic fairytale and as such it works perfectly. To make the parents a vicar and his wife is an interesting touch because it adds an extra element of conflict. Looked at as a whole, I enjoyed this and I wish you luck with it.

~ MLT

Philip, I've awarded you five points for 'Themes and Ideas'. You have so many. They have originality and are unique. I found reading them thought-provoking which is probably what you intended. I think you have succeeded in mastering the format, and therefore, perhaps, no real alterations should be made.

Incidentally, I found the book jacket illustration extremely interesting. It projects the heart of the story without making it too obvious. Maybe I should have said 'belly button' of the story.

I wish I could give more constructive criticism, but I feel I might mislead you into unnecessary alterations.

~ Hermit

Contents

Λ Broken Dream

Once upon a time, when dreaming was useful, a child was born. His father, with youthful exuberance, watched his son enter his world and exclaimed, "Oh, me God, he's beautiful! He's ..." He stopped exclaiming for he had seen something he had not expected. His silence was palpable as he frowned and quickly forced a smile back to his face. Too late. His straining wife, focused on her own exertions, pains and joys, sensed a peripheral shiver touch her heart. She looked at her husband's wooden smile and knew all was not well. The midwife and her two assistants – village girls learning this important craft – caught the cool wind of concern and they stopped momentarily, uneasily, for a second that travelled into eternity.

An impartial observer would have sensed nothing but, for those involved, a ripple of time, a shadow of unease, passed through all of them. They then returned to what needed to be done, pretending they had not seen what was fully evident.

The naked wee babe was wiped of the wax over his pink body with damp cloths infused with herbs, and then placed on his mother's naked belly, flesh to flesh. Her fervent panting had by now given way to gentle sighs and grateful smiles and all looked a picture of peace as the three other women gathered their ewers, bowls, utensils and unused liquids, to be cleansed or buried in the ancient way. They left the candles burning and the bundles of sage and lavender smouldering to help cleanse and purify the room.

The young druid[1], his wife and son were soon alone. As he sat smiling at his wife and child, he wondered why the Goddess, The Mother, would give him perfection in everything and then mar it with deformity. He considered whether he should rewrite tomorrow's sermon which was written, in anticipation of this sweet moment, on the Goddess's preference for providing us with perfection if we would but get out of His way, stop judging and love what is provided. Perhaps the point is to accept perfection and imperfection, beauty and deformity, for life was never perfect, easy and fully joyous. Lovely sentiments, nice theory for a priest to talk about but, blast it! This was his son, in his life, in his house and they'd all have to live with that abnormality, that un-human monstrosity, forever. It just wasn't fair, especially for a man of the Goddess to have to deal with the cruel humour of a vicious creator.

---

(1) The word *Druid* is purely Celtic and its meaning probably implies that, like the sorcerer and medicine-man everywhere, the Druid was regarded as "the knowing one." It is composed of two parts - dru (an intensive) and vids, from vid, "to know," or "see." Hence the Druid was "the very knowing or wise one." It is possible, however, that dru- is connected with the root which gives the word "oak" in Celtic speech - Gaulish deruo, Irish dair, Welsh derw - and that the oak, occupying a place in the cult, was thus brought into relation with the name of the priesthood. The Gaulish form of the name was probably druis, the Old Irish was drai. The modern forms in Irish and Scots Gaelic, drui and draoi, mean "sorcerer."

(2) Gutuatri is the equivalent of a Druidic High Priest.

The Goddess had always been so loving till now so why did She have to turn on him, a good and pious man who had given his life over to Her and Her mighty works and now, now that he had all he wanted, She savagely distorts that which he must live with. Why, oh why, Dear Goddess? Why me? Why now? His thoughts raged on.

The dread that had been instilled in his heart from the gathering of men of his calling, two valleys away, two moons ago, rose as bile in his throat. In their flowing white cloaks the men had stepped down into their sacred pit, inside the heart of The Mother, to hear The Mother speak to them through the voice of their gutuatri[2]. Instead of uplifting, the words were, this time, quietly foreboding of a time to come. This End Time, The Mother said, would see neighbour fight with neighbour, famine would be on the land and peoples' minds and bodies would be deformed. This Time, She said, may not be in their lifetimes and they must not talk of it to the uninitiated, to the villagers. In fact, She said, the priests must bring as much light and love to their people for that could, perhaps, keep the blackness from this land. It would, at least, reduce its tragic effects.

This message of doom, though a long time off, had shaken Bryn to his bones and he could not share it with anyone and so it grew. And now his son – his son, the son of a druid priest – was deformed. Was it a reflection of his own impurity, the ungodliness he kept inside? He felt The Mother pointing at him, not with her usually loving smile but with an accusing grimace.

He knew that the deformity was there – he had seen it – but it was now hidden, pressed against his wife's soft belly. He felt himself slipping off the map of his life, his fingers clinging to the edge as pebbles loosened themselves and spun into the abyss below. This was not as he had planned it to be and now he could feel himself about to plummet into the rude forests of his ancestors where gnarly, savage creatures waited to taunt him, if not to devour him. As that ancient fear of all men – the fear of not being in control – threatened to swamp him, he remembered his training. So he invited the Goddess inside. He sat with Her inside. He stilled his mind, opened his palms, softened his jaw and smiled his eyes and mouth. He crawled back from that cracking edge of a life so-dreamed and lay there panting on the warm earth as She stilled his rushing thoughts. Through the panic he arrived back home to a comfortable peace, a knowing that he knew nothing, and that was as it should be, somehow.

He smiled an easy smile now and his young wife opened her eyes at its invitation. At the instant that she had first seen the uncertainty and fear in her husband's eyes, as their child entered his new world, she had shut the doors of doubt and cocooned herself in that sweet and primitive first moment of embrace with what had been inside her, returning to her as the perfect embodiment of their love. This moment would never come again and her bliss kept the dark wolves of doubt far from her door.

The Wolves Wait Still

Time passes in this world and we must move on or be swallowed by the giant of indolence. We have our dreaming but we must awake, face the rising sun and return to the world of sharp edges and defined tasks.

Her husband's soft smile was the rising sun she woke to and, despite his easy manner and loving looks, she knew there were going to be sharp edges and defined tasks to encounter this day. Many, probably.

"What is yer concern, Bryn?" she asked.

"Hold our baby up and ye will see, Eryn," he said, not daring to move a muscle. She did so and gasped.

"Oh, Bryn, that be amazing!" she exclaimed.

"Amazing? It be ugly!" said Bryn, grimacing.

"No, not ugly, husband, not ugly at all," said Eryn, looking at him softly. "It be different, it be ... um, unexpected, but it not be ugly at all."

"It's not normal, not normal at all," said Bryn, remaining very still, attempting to control his emotions with his muscles.

"Oh Bryn, me husband, ye be disappointed, let down, for ye wanted to have ye own kind of perfection, not God's."

"But that be not human, not normal. Humans have flesh there. They have, um, belly buttons of flesh," said

Bryn, daring himself to ease forward to take a closer look.

"Well, yes, I be surprised, shocked even," said Eryn, considering her son's belly button. "But no matter how I try, I cannot see ugly. I just cannot see that."

"But it's not normal. What will we tell people? What will they think of a priest's son with a golden belly button? We'll be laughing stocks. He'll be ostracised ..."

"Bryn! Bryn, Bryn, me darling man. Go quietly for a moment now," said Eryn, trying to soothe his turbulent waters. "What other people make of it is what we make of it. And if they don't, they'll make of it what they will anyway."

"People will see this deformity," said Bryn, sitting back and closing his eyes to keep the crowd scene out of his mind, unsuccessfully.

"Bryn me love, this is our son and he has what he has. We have what we have – a son with a golden belly button," said Eryn, holding her little boy closer while stroking his shiny belly button. "He has what he has and we have what we have. Would ye have us throw him out with the rubbish? Feed him to the wolves?"

"No! No me love, of course not!" said Bryn, reaching forward and touching her arm. He realised, in that moment, he was unable to touch his son and an ice shard stabbed his heart as he thought on that. "We have him but ... but, oh, I don't know. I just don't know."

"But ye do know, Bryn. Ye know quite well," said Eryn, smiling at him. "Ye asked God, with all yer fervent might, for a perfect son who was special. I heard ye, many times, asking for such. And I agreed with ye. I wanted that too. We asked God and God delivered our desire."

"But I didna' want summat inhuman," said Bryn, wiping the back of his hand over his forehead. Tears were forming but he was just not going to acknowledge them with a wipe.

"Me darling sweet Man of God, do ye not see?" asked Eryn hugging the sweet child asleep in her arms, oblivious of the talking about him. "He is perfect. He is special. We got what we asked of God. Do ye not see? If he is of God, from God, then nothing but good can come of this. Nothing but good."

"Nothing but good for a child with a deformity!" said Bryn, leaning forward, his hands clenched. "How can that ever be?"

"We donna' know how God makes a golden belly button – we certainly cannot," said Eryn evenly. "So if we leave the rest, the future, in the hands of God, we canna' know, right now, how he makes the goodness come of it but we know he can. It not be our job to know how but our job to believe how. Isna' that what ye tell the villagers in yer sermons?"

"Hmph! That be the problem with being a priest," he said. "I might be knowin' all the scripture and all the wise words known to man and I can tell them to those who canna' read them. But once they're out of me mouth, in public, people expect me to live them, to know how to deal with all of life's challenges. And, quite frankly, Eryn, me wise woman, I feel like I know nothing."

"But me darling man," she said, patting his arm. "Ye' be honest about yer not knowing and ye be sincerely trying to live as a good Man of God."

"Ye have faith in me that's higher than mine, Eryn!" he said, chuckling and sitting back. "It's almost that I used to know so much and, as I grow older, I grow dimmer. I talk the words and ye live them – ye should be the priest!"

"We make a good team, then!" said Eryn, laughing. "Betwixt me wise doing and yer wise sermons we're the wisest couple that ever was."

And so their lives continued for some time, with Bryn trying to come to terms with his son having a golden belly button and with Eryn accepting the perfection and specialness of young Donal, as they called him. They agreed – till they heard differently and clearly from God – to do or say nothing about Donal's golden belly button and to keep it covered at all times. Living in the public eye and in a public place – a priest's home was a sanctuary for anyone needing succour, physical or spiritual – they had to be ever vigilant. That wasn't always easy. The midwife and her three apprentices had seen but their calling swore them to tell nothing of the births they attended. Birth was a sacred and private process and they kept their sworn vows.

Love's Demands

Despite the strain of keeping Donal's secret, his parents maintained the outward appearance of normality and kept their inner turmoil to themselves.

It's a strange irony: the less we talk about something, the bigger it gets.

And so it was with Donal, a happy wee toddler. Beneath that happiness was a concern, as the flutter of an autumn leaf about to die, but never quite does. This gentle leaf would waft by his mind, touch it in the softest way and glide on to return the next hour, the next day or the next week. Sometimes, in the middle of play or some other activity he would stop and sense something ... an unease, a doubt, a gap in his happiness. While his face displayed an ever-present smile, that fluttering leaf of autumn threatened to bring in the chill of winter, but never quite did.

Donal's parents were afeared that another child of theirs would be cursed and so they strongly resisted their deepest desire – another wee child. However, as is the way of people to find love within and evil without, a child was conceived and was born two years after Donal was received as a gift from The Mother.

Donal had so wanted to see his new friend arrive but he was kept from the house, at his father's request, lest he contaminate the purity of the new babe within. When

Donal did finally see his new brother, Ianto, he was over-come by the beauty and just wanted to hold him and stare at him. His father forbade that and Donal was kept across the room, puzzled, sad and yearning. He felt he saw a sad-ness on his mother's face as his father pushed him back but she complied with her husband's fears.

Some time later, after his father had gone out to min-ister to the sick, his mother had beckoned him over. Confused and reluctant to disobey his father, he faltered.

"Oh Donal, I'm so sorry," said his mother, pleading. "I know ye so want to hold and love yer brother. Come here, me dear son."

Donal approached his mother and the wee bundle on her knee. He felt tears welling up and his mother grabbed him to her bosom and they cried quietly together, with Ianto sleeping between them.

As he grew and as the silence around his specialness grew, so did the feeling that there was something wrong with him, that he wasn't good enough. This bouncing toddler was unaware of it, of course, but the seeds of doubt and fear, sown at his birth, etched themselves ev-er-so-gently into his soul. These seeds were watered by the sideways looks of his parents, sometimes, especially of his father. They were fertilized by the furtive conver-sations of his parents when they thought he was out of earshot. And, more than ever, they were nurtured by the heavy silence, the secret-holding that surrounded him.

No one had told Donal this but he just knew it ... or maybe he had just made it up. Or maybe he was wrong. However it came into his head, there it was, this constant thought that all of life should be equal, near enough. If you gave you got. If you were nice, people were nice back. If you helped someone, someone helped you back.

That wasn't why he gave, was nice and helped – he

did that because it felt good and right – but it jarred in his thoughts when life didn't show itself as equal. His sense of balance walked away at these times.

He did think, many times, that this thought might be wrong. But, no matter how many times it was broken, violated, the thought stayed in his mind that this is the way life should be – balanced, equal and fair.

It mystified Donal greatly that he would do things for his brother, because he loved and adored him, but his brother would do nothing for him. He reasoned that Ianto did not love and adore him and so he'd try harder, being the perfect brother, being the best friend. The harder he tried to win Ianto's affections – the more he helped and encouraged – the more was demanded of him. It was like killing flies – every time he killed one, the whole family came to the funeral. Every time he did something for Ianto, many more things arrived for him to do.

The demands did not just come from the wining maw of Ianto. His parents told him, constantly, that he was the older brother now and must look after his younger brother. It became a regular family chant and he knew he would hear it several times a day – Donal, pick up Ianto's toys; Donal, clean Ianto's face; Donal, take Ianto for a walk; Donal, it's no time to be sitting; Donal, help get Ianto dressed; Donal, help with this here; Donal, help with that there; Donal, Donal, Donal, on and on.

It all went against that big thought in his head, the thought of balance and equality, but it seemed he had no choice but disobey it and serve others. He did sometimes wonder, when he had a rare moment of peace to himself, who would help him if he was ever struggling with something.

He did, sometimes, imagine that his mother looked at him sadly – even helplessly – as he rushed from one duty to another.

At times he would ask, with feelings of guilt and trep-
idation, why Ianto could not clean the dishes or sweep
the floor or feed the chickens and, each time, he would
be told that Ianto was too small at the moment and that
he would do those things when he was bigger. Years later,
when Ianto was bigger, he would ask if it was Ianto's turn
to do things and he would be told that as he was so good
at them now, he may as well carry on doing them. Donal
could never find an answer to such illogical statements
and so he would bow his head, carry on with his work and
creep back into his beautifully free world of imagination.
In this wondrous world he would be unbothered by people
and he and his Imaginary Friend would create magical
experiences and places with the waggle of a finger. There
would be no cleaning or sweeping or feeding or chopping
or mending or errands. A finger waggle would have his
world perfect, as he wanted it, never dirty or falling into
disrepair in the way that silly other world did.

The best thing about this imaginary world was that he
was not involved, not commanded. There were nice people around but they did not bother him, did not demand of
him, did not berate him. He could listen to their problems
but he didn't have to do anything about them. They felt
better by being listened to and he made them feel better
quite effortlessly. In fact, in this magical world of his imagination, with his Imaginary Friend, it seemed like the
less he did, the happier people were … quite the opposite
of the other demanding one.

Little did Donal know that by imagining this effortless
and beautiful world, with such love and passion, he was
starting to create the reality of it.

A Story Discovers Itself

He soon found a story discovering itself inside him; a story that told him that his parents weren't quite on his side. As their whispered conversations – obviously about him – increased, so did the story that talked to him. His parents were nice. They were friendly. They were fun, sometimes. They got him lots of things. But they whispered about him and kept their secrets. As they hid a little of themselves from him, so did he hide a little of himself from them. He learned, from his story, how to keep his real self protected, hidden. Whether he was happy or sad, lonely or peaceful, his parents saw a happy little man.

The trust that may have been there at his birth slowly dissolved and he began to feel alone in the world. He retreated into his story, his only real friend. As the whisperings and late-night arguments about him grew, so did his story. Behind the story, he realised, was an angel telling it and that angel became his friend.

Then, the inevitable happened. His parents were very careful to keep his tummy covered at all times and to keep him as inactive as possible – no climbing trees, no running fast, no little-boy stuff. But we all know about little boys and their stuff, don't we? They are built with tough springs and other machinery that has them leaping about, exploring their world, challenging their world, challenging themselves. They love doing all that with other little boys. No matter how much cosseting the parents indulge in, a little boy's machinery has a monster magnet in its centre and it attracts other little boys who like doing little boy things. Yes, his internal little-boy machinery inevitably drew in two other little boys, walking along his lane and, whoosh!, they were in his yard, chatting with him, playing with him. Soon enough they were having a climbing competition to get to the top of the stone wall around his house. Yes, well, boys are meant to fall from things (like stone walls) and to bounce. Mothers don't understand this as they are girls and girls don't bounce, they hurt. Mothers don't understand that boys bounce but they do. When it was his turn to accidentally fall (every boy must have a turn at accidentally falling), as his two friends had, he bounced on the grass and lay there laughing. He hadn't thrown his body about before and he felt a great surge of freedom. He loved it.

His mother chanced to see him fall and her instinct was to rush out and pick him up. However, when the universe is determined that something will happen, it has its way. His mother faltered, waited, forced herself to breathe and prayed he would be alright. In that faltering instant, his shirt came out of his breeches (as the universe decreed) and his two friends saw something they hadn't seen before – a wondrous sight!

"Ooo, what's that? It be shiny," said Marcus.

"That yers? It be odd," said Sean.

"This mine. What's yers?" asked Donal.

The two boys stood where they were, on top of the wall, lifted their shirts up and showed him their fleshy belly buttons.

As is the way with all little boys with golden belly buttons (who thought every other boy had one) he was speechless, rooted to the spot. Two against one and he was the one to be different. The other two boys, secure in the knowing that they were usual, normal, were curious and then other curiosities took their attention, like how high up the wall could they jump from. Donal tried to join in to look as normal as possible and, to his worried mother, it looked as if the momentary freeze-frame of her worst fear almost never happened – a fleeting flash of gold, inquisitive looks and then on to the next adventure.

Not so for Donal. He immediately knew he was odd and nothing could take back that moment. He was stuck, doomed and forever ... ah, different. To have not continued romping with the normal boys would have made his difference even greater so he leapt up as if nothing had happened and joined in the fun. In fact, he was not to be outdone, jumping from the highest, running the fastest and being the funniest. His new difference gave him wings while others had only legs.

In the wisp of that moment, forgotten by others, was born the urge to excel and, hence, to expel any difference that may be perceived, no matter how tangible and permanent it may be. In that moment, a new Donal was born ... actually, in that moment, a Donal died and two new Donals were born. The normally-happy-but-slightly-sad Donal was no more and in his place there appeared, like the hydra's head, two quite divergent Donals.

One was aghast, shocked and saddened at his relegation to the underworld of the dark monsters of not fitting in, with the cavernous jaws of flame and censure ever ready to devour him. There was nothing to be done but keep running, for the dark creatures of judgement – all scaly skin and hacking claws – had no compassion or reasoning and could never be mollified. So Donal II lived in constant fear, his mind crashing through the dark forests of his ancestors, not knowing how to stop or where he was going.

And Donal III? Well, he was the body in the bright world of sunshine, the successful, glorious achiever who wowed and amazed all he met. While Donal II was furiously paddling in circles, Donal III was gliding effortlessly with a smile and sure direction.

So Donal went both up and down, with nothing for the middle way. The spectre of being different sent Donal II underground and Donal III to the heavens.

Donal II took to walking beneath the mushroom stalks, with the moles and badgers. The light of day and the busyness of the world never stirred down here. All was quiet, warm and safe. However, though the creatures were gentle and friendly, they weren't people.

Meanwhile, Donal III took on the world with a flourish and excelled in everything he needed to. Though humans were around him, in admiration, none were there with him or for him. Or so he felt.

He stopped telling his mother the little secrets a little boy tells his mother. He stopped sitting and walking with his father, as a boy is proudly inclined to do.

His father's calling thrust the family to the forefront of village life and Donal performed where he must. He developed the most beautiful of voices in the choir and his voice, soaring above the harmonies below, brought one to tears and smiles. Though his father resisted making him the head chorister, for fear of favouritism, Donal's talent made it impossible for resistance to last very long. So he would sing, impress and move people and, after the service, would disappear out the back door and go home or to the woods alone.

The horse was the only means of transport and, like all necessities, he deemed that he must be supreme on his pony. At the village fetes and county fares he would perform with daring, skill and grace – the envy of the men and the adoration of the women. After he had vanquished the competitors on horseback and the women in their hearts, he would suddenly be gone, like the mist in the morning sun. Many might want to shake his hand or touch him sweetly but, already, he had vanished to be alone.

We don't know if word got around about his golden belly button and nor did he. But ye and I, like him, must assume that the stories flew about that he was not altogether normal; that he was special, different, odd and apart from mere mortals. Taking himself into aloneness kept the noise of those chattering tongues from his ears, kept the awkward questions away and, most frightening of all, kept away those who might ask to see his mark of difference. It must be hidden, at all costs, and so he took it with him to the dark and quiet places people would never be.

In the woods or the barren heaths he would make friends with animals, birds and insects, with his trusty pony beneath him. His greatest friend, that quiet inner voice that grew into an angel, was with him whether running away from or at the world. He was much comforted by the words of reassurance and support his angel uttered and, with that kind being, he thought he'd never be sad or alone.

But he was, he discovered.

It touched him in the pit of his soul, just behind the golden belly button. At first, he didn't notice it. It continued to grow from a dim murmur, once in a while, to a constant gnawing that could not be ignored. He finally had to acknowledge it, one day, and it did hurt. Its tentacles reached down to his bowels and up around his heart, making his heart a little heavier each day.

He asked his angel, constantly, for help with this deep angst, this slowly growing pain, and he heard no answer. Ye and I know that the angel did answer but he was deaf to that which he did not want to hear.

Sage Of Silence

I n the village of Golden Valley ... indeed, in all villages of the Golden Valley and probably beyond but no one knew as none ventured that far ... those with Golden Fingers held a special place in peoples' hearts. Some of these Golden Fingers were attached to gnarled hands and hefty arms and were suited to farming tasks like ploughing, wall-building and shearing. Some Golden Fingers were attached to accurate hands and strong arms and could carve fine furniture, musical instruments and ornaments. Some Golden Fingers flew along hemlines and through button-holes with scissors, needle and thread. The tasks these Golden Fingers found themselves enjoying were tasks born into them at birth ... probably before birth, for all we know ... and the sinews, muscles and bones knew of their tasks before a baby's first fist-clench.

Those whose fingers were more leaden than golden lived at the bottom of the heap unless they had been gifted Golden Brains and could lead the village pries[3], as Donal's father did. Donal had a Golden Voice but no Golden Fingers or Brains ... or so no one could discern. As you know, brains can only be judged by those wise enough to set brain tests and, as there was no one possessed of such cleverness in Nantwich of Golden Valley,

---

(3) Pries = prayers

Donal could not be tested and so his brain was deemed to be as dim as each person judging its cleverness.

So, in the village of Nantwich, where there were Golden Fingers and one Golden Brain (his father, who dared not suggest a pedestal for his son) Donal was thought to have no talents save for that of his voice which, as all knew, was no talent at all as it neither sheltered, fed nor saved anyone from anything.

He had reached the ripe young age of sixteen when young men are captivated by the ripening bodies of young women and by the prospect of entering the world of men. It is a time when they must divorce their parents and marry their peers, hanging about in groups pretending to be those they have recently divorced. With all the answers to the ills of the world, they so clearly see the stupidity of their parents and clamour for change in everything. But Donal knew little, if anything, of this, and he wondered what the older boys were doing, laughing and strutting amongst themselves while groups of girls did the same in their particularly girly ways. He wondered at the way boys and girls looked at each other oddly, smiling stupidly, while he passed by to his sanctuary of the sweet and silent hills.

He had long since divorced his parents while still living with them in the same house. Conversations were stilted, awkward, and that deeper part of him longed for his younger days when ease and happiness reigned in the home. But it didn't while as his parents held doubt and uncertainty in their hearts – doubt and uncertainty about the goodness and rightness of their beautiful boy. They tried. My gosh, they tried but, no matter how hard they tried, they could not keep judgement at bay. Donal felt this though he could not put words or coherency to it. They didn't entirely accept him and so, to him, the world rejected him, though he must continue to live within its restrictive and uncomfortable walls.

Then, at this defining age of sixteen, when boys-try-ing-to-be-men must adhere themselves to an occupation, Donal took the only logical course available. With his angst fuelling the need to run, he made his decision. Against expectation, he rejected his father's calling and flew on the wind. He may have reflected, later, that he really did take his father's calling but on a horse rather that at a pulpit. Like all young people, he secretly yearned to be that which he so roundly rejected.

As we know, it is only people who are less attached to the things and relationships of this world who are able to take the biggest risks – they have little to lose and so they stride boldly where others fear to creep.

Being a minstrel, a troubadour, was seen as a risky, and therefore mysterious, vocation. Donal set forth on his pony, Toby, his only possessions attached to the saddle, in the hope of finding habitation and, moreover, habitation that housed people who were able and willing to pay him in some way.

His sustenance was meagre, at first, for he knew no stories to enchant people with. He had chosen not to ap-prentice himself to a master story-teller and, in his seclu-sion, he had learned little of the lore of his ancestors. His lack of contact with the world ensured that he learned lit-tle of the doings of ordinary and great people.

As his haphazard and hazardous journey began, he had little to recommend him but his magnificent voice and a knowing of a large number of songs to God. This did sup-port him but only just. Though there was always grass on the roadsides for Toby, he went hungry many times in his first year. Often he would be fed and sheltered, for a night, out of pity for his stupidity or his naivety.

He was a well-built and handsome lad so many a mother provided sustenance in the hope of his interest in their daughters. It was made clear that he would, however, have had to stop his wandering days to marry. This confirmed to him that he would spend his life alone.

One gift that loners develop is that of listening and this he excelled at. With few stories of his own – except his own life which he thought was uninteresting – he discovered that people were mightily entertained by being listened to. The most verbose had the smallest events to tell of while those with fascinating lives, of great intrigue and adventure, said little. This amused and bemused him and he would say to himself, "Little lives, big tongues. Big lives, little tongues!" What he didn't realise was that his silence around events of his own life lent him an aura of mystique, even majesty.

As he developed his listening skills, so he learned many stories and so his repertoire grew. But, though his head grew to bursting with fascinating, sad and hilarious anecdotes, his greatest income came from shutting his mouth and opening his ears. In this he became unique among story-tellers and his aura of mystery grew into an aura of wisdom. His beautiful singing voice – the voice of God, as many called it – and his quiet stillness let people convince themselves that he had access to knowing beyond ordinary humans.

People began to ask his advice on all manner of things: the right time for woodcutting; the number of children one might bear; the suitability of others for marriage; matters of village governance; the productivity of particular sheep; the safety of proposed business ventures; how to keep demons out of one's head or the village and so on. Of course, Donal knew nothing of these things and so he simply listened, asked questions and listened again. In time, the inquirer would come to their own conclusions, thereby crediting Donal with the amazing answer which, in time, would become a self-fulfilling prophesy. He became, after several years, famous throughout the land for the accuracy of his prophesies and people began to seek him out.

This resulted in him being showered with more coins and, when that was not available, products of his inquirers' enterprises. Carvers gave him bowls, tinkers gave him pots, fletchers gave him arrows, bodgers gave him chairs. This meant that he had to obtain for himself a cart to carry these things he had no need for. The cart was provided by a very thankful farmer when Donal touched his prize boar and, soon after, it produced many litters of piglets. His trusty pony, Toby, who he loved with much affection, was unfitted to towing a cart and another farmer who had recently, through Donal's "advice", found the courage to ask for his love's hand in marriage, successfully, provided him with a fine cart horse.

Hence, Donal's lifestyle was abruptly changed. He now had to ride on the cart while Toby, tied by the reins to the back of the cart, walked behind. His life felt suddenly cluttered, clumsy and slow. The cart would become stuck in boggy soil as Toby never had. Parts of it would break and he'd have to spend time mending it. But, worst of all, people would want to ride with him.

As he put on the attitude of singer and listener, whereby he made his growing wealth, he would feel the weight of that responsibility. He might grudgingly acknowledge that it was usually pleasant and moving and warm and amusing to be with other humans but he was always with them as a minstrel-becoming-a-sage. As such, he was always a visitor, never quite one of them, and he did have to be careful and focused. Then, each time he departed a village, he would breathe a sigh of relief – born of many year's habit – to be back on his own with his horses and the undemanding countryside to welcome him back.

Past, Soon and Now Meet

Owning a cart might seem as a blessing. However, it meant he had no excuse to keep people out of this special, secret part of his life. Feeling unable to say "no" to these gentle requests for help along the by-ways, he was always most pleasant company and listened (yet again) with rapt attention to their chattering tongues. He chafed at having to take these walkers, though most offered coins or food to pay for their fare, for he knew he could not take off his disguise of wisdom, concern and capability.

And so, on this day, it surprised him that he stopped and offered an old lady a ride – he was enjoying the solace of solitude and the gentle thud of his horses' hooves on the forest floor.

"Aye no, young man," she said, smiling up at him as she leaned on her gnarled stick. "Ye be enjoying yer own company and I no be wantin' to disturb yer soul's peace."

"But we be over a day's walk to the next village. Where will ye stay on this cold night?" he asked, wondering why he was not moving on. "I'll help ye up to take the weight from yer sodden feet."

"Are ye sure, young man?" she asked, brushing aside strands of white hair. "I fancy yer aloneness is yer heart's desire. Why would ye be wantin' to break that with an old lady?"

Donal had no answer. He just sat there on his cart, looking at her and wondering what was stopping him moving on.

"Ye see, Mr Donal ... if I may call ye that ..."

"Oh yes, that's as they call me," he said, wondering how she knew his name.

"Ye see, Mr Donal, we be always runnin' from summit but we canna' run forever," she said and an icy breeze blew down his spine. "It may be yer time, this day, to stop runnin'." This meant nothing to him but it chilled him to his bones, while strangely warming his belly at the same time. He leapt down, placed the lady's sack in the back of his cart and helped her up onto the seat at the front – not that she needed much help as she seemed as lithe and strong as a girl of twenty.

"So, me young man, Mr Donal, tell me yer story," she said as he rattled the reins and they moved forward.

"Uh, I, ah, have no story to tell, Ma'am," said Donal, feeling the hot flush of embarrassment rising through his body and face. Nobody had ever asked him that question before and he had no answer. "Ah, what am I to call ye, Ma'am?" he asked, stalling for time.

"I am, as ye know in yer heart, Morgan Pastly," said the old lady, patting his hand. He noticed, though he tried not to look surprised, a large brown circle, like a birth-mark, on the back of her left hand. He had never seen such a thing.

"Past ..." he said, feeling as if his brain was going in and out of focus, ever so slightly.

"And since ye be afraid to free the words in yer heart, I'll release them for ye," Morgan said with a pleasant chuckle. "Ye want to know how God thinks, aye?"

"Uh, ah, yes ..." he said, realising that was the one question he'd always asked when he was puzzled or pained.

"Let me tell ye from yer past, then," said Morgan, closing her eyes. The cart stopped and he listened. "Whenever ye feel pain, ye run to loneliness to feel peace and it works but a while. Every time ye find this separation, this sort-of-peace, yer talents bring ye back to people, to unity. As a child ye ran and yer voice and horse-riding brought ye back. Ye chose to be a running minstrel but yer voice and yer listening brought ye back. Ye were content for a while for ye could always escape on yer pony. Then yer talents brought this cart and people returned to ye."

"But I did none of that. It just happened to me," said Donal quietly, uneasily.

"If ye had been truly happy in yer solitude, ye would not have had it disturbed," said Morgan. "Ye kept asking how God thinks, how the universe works, for ye were not content, though ye tried to pretend ye were. And now here I am giving ye some of the answer. I must go now and leave ye to yer precious solitude." She hopped off his new cart and went to the back to fetch her bag. As he turned to plead her return, she was not there. He stood and looked all around and there were no footprints in the mud, no sounds, nothing. He sat down, stunned, and Toby walked up and nuzzled his leg.

"Yes, me friend, it can be lonely out here, can't it?" said Donal as tears freely flowed down. He untied Toby from the cart, hopped on his back and rode forward, taking Clyde's bridle. The three rode forward together till sunset.

The next morning he was up bright and early, with a strange sense of excitement and emptiness – happy and sad.

Soon, he stopped and offered an old man a ride as he pondered the strange feeling and enjoyed the gentle thud of his horses' hooves on the forest floor.

"Aye no, young man," he said, smiling up at him as he leaned on his gnarled stick. "Ye be enjoying yer own company and I no be wantin' to disturb yer soul's peace."

"But we're over a day's walk to the next village. Where will ye stay on this cold night?" he asked, wondering why he was not moving on. "I'll help ye up to take the weight from yer sodden feet."

"Are ye sure, young man?" he asked, brushing aside strands of white hair. "I fancy yer aloneness is yer heart's desire. Why would ye be wantin' to break that with an old man?"

Donal had no answer. He just sat there on his cart, looking at him.

"Ye see, Mr Donal ... if I may call ye that ..."

"Oh yes, that's as they call me," he said, wondering how he knew his name.

"Ye see, Mr Donal, we're always runnin' from summit but we canna' run forever," he said and an icy breeze blew down his spine. "It may be yer time, this day, to stop runnin'." The old man tossed his sack in the back of the cart and leapt up beside Donal with the agility of a young man.

"And yer name, old man?" asked Donal, feeling more confident than he ever had before.

"Me name, Donal lad, is Morghan Soonly," said the old man with a youthful chuckle. "And it's yer future ye be wantin' to know, I be guessing."

"Well, yes ... ah, I suppose that would be interesting," said Donal uncertainly, hopefully, not wanting give into the joyful little spark in his belly, lit by Morghan's question. For the first time ever, he really did want to peer down the dark tunnel of his life-to-come and see if there was any light at the end.

"Let me tell yer then. There's no future, Donal boy, for ye or anyone else," said Morghan, patting Donal's hand as

Clyde stopped ... the world stopped. Donal noticed a large birth mark on the back of Morghan's left hand. "There is only now. Where ye want to be in yer next now is written not in the stars but in yer little willingness, in the pounding heart of yer desire to be more than ye are now."

"Me little willingness?" asked Donal, confused and curious.

"Let me say it this way, me friend," said Morghan, turning to face Donal. "I did not turn up unexpectedly today – ye called me up, just as ye called up every other person, event and feeling. Ye be driving the cart of yer life – not the other way around."

"Um, I suppose so," said Donal, not knowing what to say or think next as he urged Clyde on again. "Yer hand ... uh, what's that mark?"

"Ah, just a birthmark. We've all got something to get over," said Morghan, dismissively. "Ye see, whatever we think holds us back is what we be here to do, to succeed through. Yers is to let out all the feelings, good and bad, from yer belly, tell yer story, sing yer story and inspire those who be afraid of their inner feelings. Let it out. Let it shine, me lad!"

Donal quickly thought of his shiny belly button and smiled stupidly.

"And now I go," said Morghan at no place in particular in the woods. "Let it shine, me friend!" Morghan hopped off, took a step back to grab his sack and was gone. Not there. Not anywhere.

Donal sat and smiled. The sun was starting to shine in his mind. He knew not what Morghan had said but, somehow he did. Toby whinnied and trotted forward to nuzzle his leg. Clyde shook himself happily and the cart and leathers all rattled.

"Yes, it's time for us to be free!" said Donal as he leapt

down to untie the horses. He felt quite young again and leaned back against an old oak and looked up at the brightening sky while the horses foraged for tasty morsels.

Morganna

The next morning dawned warm and still and the feeling of lightness had dimmed. He was between his old feelings of dread and the new feeling of joy, afraid the joy would disappear. Clyde was by the cart, ready to be tied in and he left Toby loose, to wander with him unfettered. Uncertain of the coming day's events, he made himself smile and prayed to his angel for hope.

As it turned out, the day was long and uneventful. He was sure he'd lost his way, though he'd been this way many times before. It was late afternoon that the track widened and told of a settlement ahead. Ahead was a young lady, a creature he had more fear of than any other. He needed to keep going for the village was not far and he was out of food. With heart in mouth, he stopped by the lass and asked her if she would like to ride in the cart.

"Why, thank ye, Sir," she said brightly. "I be travelling many a year and I really do need to stop." She leapt up and tossed her small sack into the back of the cart.

Donal sneaked a look at her face and his mouth fell open. There was no mistaking it – she was the likeness of the angel who had been at his side these past ten years.

"Oh dear, do I look so dreadful?" asked the lass, looking worried. "Ye be not frightened of me, are ye?"

"No ... ah, no, not at all," said Donal, not knowing where to start explaining. "It's just ... just that ye look like me ... ah, someone I know. What name are ye called by, then?" he asked while his mind tried to find something else to say.

"I be Morganna. What be yer name, sir?" she asked.

"Oh, gosh ..."

"Gosh, what an unusual name. Are ye from foreign parts?" Morganna asked, smiling. Her smile warmed his uncertainty. He thought she was joking but he wasn't sure.

"Ah, no, I'm er, I be called Donal," he said, almost forgetting his own name.

"Oh me gosh!" she said.

"No, Donal ..." he said.

"Yes, yes, I know," she said quickly. "I only said 'oh gosh' as I hadn't heard that name before, except in me special conversations."

"Special conversations?" asked Donal.

"Oh dear, ye'll think me a silly girl, now won't ye," she said, blushing. "Oh well, I'll tell ye then since I've started. I have this person I speak to, this man who used to be a boy but grew up and, well, his name is Donal, just like yers."

"So I'm not the only one!" he said, clapping his hand to his head. "Ye have a secret voice, an angel too?"

"And ye have one too?" she asked, wide-eyed. "What be his name?"

"Actually, he has no name ... it's a she and she's the likeness of ye, just like ye!" he said, feeling the shard of ice around his heart beginning to melt. It felt like his belly button was laughing. They both sat and looked at each other, unable to find or form words. After a moment, she broke the spell.

"It's a warm day, isn't it," she said as she struggled out of her overcoat. As she did so, her shirt came out of her breeches a little and he spied two golden rings, pierced through her belly button. "Oh!" she said, embarrassed and tucked her shirt in again.

"A golden belly button ..." said Donal quietly.

"Yes, I've always wanted a golden belly button but the rings will have to do!" she said happily. "Not sure why but that's what I've always wanted. Silly huh?"

"Maybe we *can* have what we ask for," he said, smiling his silly smile.

"Oh absolutely!" she said, patting his leg.

They smiled at each other as he urged Clyde to start for the village. He shyly put his hand on hers and she didn't move it away.

How this story came upon me

In 2010 (it may have been around May) I discovered a short-story writing competition. Now, usually, short stories are considered to be under 3,000 words (sometimes less) but this competition was different – it celebrated a writer (whose name eludes me right now) who broke the rules and wrote long short stories – and the maximum length for this competition was 7,000 words. And I so love people who break the rules!

So, with two weeks to go to deadline, I wrote a short story and sent it off. And, no, I did not win the competition … or even come second or third or anything else – you would have heard the shouting from where you live, wherever that is. However, my lovely, intelligent and discerning wife (Anna) told me that it was a beautifully written story and that I should keep writing and stretch it into a book. Well, of course, her opinion holds more weight than some silly writing judge's and so I kept writing and a novel is emerging from my busy pen.

So, what you have here is a lovely, moving story (per Anna's considered opinion) of 9,000 words and the other 90,000 words will be added over the next little while.

So now you know the story of the story. Interesting, huh?

About the Author

In New Zealand I experienced life as an accountant, credit manager, company director, shepherd, scrub-cutter, tree pruner, freezing worker, plastics factory worker, saxophonist, army driver, tour bus driver, stage and television actor and singer, builder, lecturer, facilitator for men's groups, reporter, columnist, magazine editor, publisher, writer ...

In South Africa as an AIDS workshop co-facilitator ...

In the Australian bush as a barman, horse and camel trekker and stock-whip teacher ...

In England as a contract accountant, corporate trainer, estate manager, lecturer, singer/songwriter, website editor/writer and freelance writer ...

Now that I'm back in Australia, house renovating, teaching and writing, I'm wondering what's next!

The constant for my wife and I is *A Course in Miracles*, a psychological life-style course in forgiveness. Through it I have found the peace I had always been searching for - the journey to where we have always been.

Social media contacts

About Me: https://about.me/philipbradbury
Amazon: amzn.to/25X0CLb
Facebook:
   https://www.facebook.com/
AuthorPhilipJBradbury/
Google+: http://bit.ly/2bsbpUy
Linked In - http://bit.ly/2aTzZMS
Pininterest: https://au.pinterest.com/bradburywords/
Smashwords: http://bit.ly/2aNjkic
Twitter: https://twitter.com/PhilipJBradbury
Website: www.philipjbradbury.com
Wordpress blogs:
   https://flashfictionfanatic.wordpress.com/
   https://pjbradbury.wordpress.com/

Other books by Philip J Bradbury

Non-Fiction
Life Rejuvenated
Whose Life Is It Anyway?
The Lawless Way
Change Your Life, Change Your World
The Twelve Week Miracle (with Anna Bradbury)
Understanding Men
Articles of Faith
Conversations on Your Business
Stepping Out Of Debt and Into Financial Freedom

Some-Fiction
Dactionary – the dictionary with attitude
The Meaning of Larf
53 SMILES
97 SMILES

Fiction
The Last Stand Down
An Olympic Challenge
The Royal Bank of Stories
Gerald the Great of Gorokoland

For more information on books, see ***www.***
philipjbradbury.com

Deep Gratitude to ...

You, dear reader for, without you, purchasing and recommending this book, there would be no book to purchase and recommend or to read and enjoy.

My wife Anna. She is my best friend and greatest inspiration and I thank her from the bottom of my beating heart for being there, for loving me and for being that which I wish for myself.

Anna also edited this book with her razor eye for the details I didn't see.

I started meditating in 1993 and, from that, I've been able to create miniscule spaces between my thoughts, spaces that allow God in. You see, us writers don't actually write - we just transcribe what God writes in our mind spaces, if we humble ourselves to ever leave openness for Them. So, my deep gratitude is to God - or whatever it is that's bigger than us (probably our larger, more knowing selves) - for the peace that comes from receiving and transcribing Their thoughts is indescribable.

I am also indebted to *A Course in Miracles* - and all the people I have met through it - for it shows me the way to peace; that way that is both simple and difficult. Forgiveness is simple to do, if we have a little willingness, but it's difficult to do in every second of our lives ... even when we're willing.

I keep trying ...